Illinois
America's Favorite Ghost Town!
43 Old Cemetery Road
Hospital
Library
Café
Courthouse
Lock & Key
Newspaper

43 Old Cemetery Road: Book Two

OVER MY DEAD BODY

Kate Klise

Illustrated by

M. Sarah Klise

Harcourt
Houghton Mifflin Harcourt
BOSTON NEW YORK 2009

Harcourt is an imprint of Houghton Mifflin Harcourt Publishing Company.

www.hmhbooks.com

Library of Congress Cataloging-in-Publication Data
Klise, Kate.
Over my dead body / by Kate Klise ; illustrated by M. Sarah Klise.
p. cm.
Summary: In this story told mostly through letters, busybody Dick Tater tries to ban Halloween and ghost stories, as well as to break up the popular writing team of I. B. Grumply, ghost Olive C. Spence, and eleven-year-old illustrator Seymour Hope.
ISBN 978-0-15-205734-3
[1. Authors—Fiction. 2. Books and reading—Fiction. 3. Ghosts—Fiction. 4. Haunted houses—Fiction. 5. Halloween—Fiction. 6. Letters—Fiction. 7. Humorous stories.] I. Klise, M. Sarah, ill. II. Title.
PZ7.K684Ove 2009
[Fic]—dc22
2009007979

Designed by M. Sarah Klise

Printed in the United States of America

MP 10 9 8 7 6 5 4 3 2 1

This book is dedicated
to Desmond Moss Augustine
with much 12-15-22-5.

A Warning to Readers!

This book contains material that could be considered objectionable.
Some readers might try to ban this book after turning the last page.
Others might want to ban it without even opening it.

If, while reading this book, you feel
bothered,
bewildered,
insulted,
offended,
outraged,
scandalized,
threatened,
and/or inexplicably itchy,
we apologize for the inconvenience.
Kindly return the book to the nearest bookshelf
so that someone else might enjoy this

TRUE GHOST STORY,

which begins
as soon as you
turn this
page.

Welcome to 43 Old Cemetery Road

If this is the first you've heard of 43 Old Cemetery Road, you should be aware of the following facts:

43 Old Cemetery Road is the address of a 32½-room house in Ghastly, Illinois.

Some people call the house Spence Mansion because it was built in 1874 by Olive C. Spence.

Miss Spence was an elegant woman who spent her life writing and illustrating mysteries.

But no one ever read her mysteries—except the hundreds of publishers who rejected them.

Shortly before her death, Olive C. Spence made a solemn vow to haunt her house and the town of Ghastly, Illinois, forever—or until one of her mysteries was published.

And haunt it she did. From stealing muffins to borrowing library books, Olive made her presence known. From time to time, she even appeared in an old mirror at Ghastly Antiques.
(Attempts to photograph Olive's image were never successful.)
More than 80 years after Spence's death, Les and Diane Hope bought Spence Mansion.
The Hopes were professors of the paranormal. They hoped to document the ghost of Olive C. Spence and make a lot of money off their research.
But Olive refused to cooperate. For 12 long years, she declined to have any contact with Professors Les and Diane Hope.
Why? Because she thought they were greedy.

Olive was right.

But as so often happens with wretched adults, Les and Diane Hope had a perfectly wonderful son named Seymour, who was born at Spence Mansion.

(← That's Seymour's cat. His name is Shadow.)

Seymour Hope and Olive C. Spence quickly became best friends.

Olive and Seymour also (after a somewhat rocky start) became friends with Ignatius B. Grumply, a famous author who rented Spence Mansion during the summer Les and Diane Hope abandoned Seymour.

Together, Ignatius B. Grumply, Olive C. Spence, and Seymour Hope collaborated on the first three chapters of a ghost story, which they called *43 Old Cemetery Road*. Ignatius and Olive wrote the words; Seymour drew the pictures.

They gave away
the first three chapters
of the book and
asked anyone who
wanted to read more
chapters to kindly
send $3 to
43 Old Cemetery Road.
Well, *everyone*,
it seemed, wanted to read more.
Ignatius, Olive, and Seymour
were delighted by the thousands
of orders they received from
all over the world.
The money was nice, too.
Seymour used part of it to buy
Spence Mansion from his parents,
who preferred living without him
in a hotel in Paris.
(Yes, some parents *really* are *that* awful.)
And Ignatius and Olive really were
much nicer—even though Ignatius
did get a bit grumpy now and then
when he got writer's block.
And some-
times Olive
was cranky,
especially
when she
misplaced
her reading
glasses.
But other than that, everything at
43 Old Cemetery Road was frighteningly perfect until one
day in September, when the following letter arrived . . .

INTERNATIONAL MOVEMENT FOR THE SAFETY & PROTECTION OF OUR KIDS & YOUTH

2 BUREAUCRACY AVENUE **WASHINGTON, D.C. 20505**

Dick Tater
Director

September 5

Ignatius B. Grumply
43 Old Cemetery Road
Ghastly, Illinois

Dear Mr. Grumply,

It has come to my attention that Seymour Hope is living with you in a domicile without the benefit of his parents.

As director of the International Movement for the Safety & Protection Of Our Kids & Youth (IMSPOOKY), it is my duty to see that every child in the world is protected from dangerous people, circumstances, and ideas.

Please submit a letter explaining by what authority you are caring for Seymour Hope. Are you a relative, the boy's legal guardian, or a hired caregiver?

Also, I understand that Seymour Hope has not yet reported for school this year. Please explain that, too.

Authoritatively,

Dick Tater

Dick Tater

IGNATIUS B. GRUMPLY

A WRITER IN RESIDENCE

43 OLD CEMETERY ROAD   2ND FLOOR   GHASTLY, ILLINOIS

September 9

Dick Tater
Director, IMSPOOKY
2 Bureaucracy Avenue
Washington, D.C. 20505

Dear Mr. Tater,

I'm neither Seymour's relative nor his legal guardian nor a hired caregiver. I simply found the boy in Spence Mansion, an old house I rented for the summer. Through an odd clause in the lease, I acquired the boy from his parents, who abandoned him three months ago when they left on a lecture tour of Europe.

Since then, Seymour has been happily living here with Olive C. Spence and me. Together we've formed a publishing company. Our specialty? Ghost stories.

I'll admit I had very little experience caring for children before I moved to Spence Mansion. I'll further admit I didn't even *like* children. But I'm learning from Olive. She's a wonderful mother figure for Seymour, who I'm happy to report is safe and happy at 43 Old Cemetery Road.

As for school, Seymour has asked to be homeschooled by Olive and me. I can't think of a finer education for an 11-year-old artist than illustrating ghost stories.

If you have any more questions, please don't hesitate to contact me.

Yours in the written word,

Ignatius B. Grumply

Ignatius B. Grumply

INTERNATIONAL MOVEMENT FOR THE SAFETY & PROTECTION OF OUR KIDS & YOUTH

2 BUREAUCRACY AVENUE **WASHINGTON, D.C. 20505**

Dick Tater
Director

September 12

Ignatius B. Grumply
43 Old Cemetery Road
Ghastly, Illinois

Dear Mr. Grumply,

You cannot legally "acquire" a child through a rental lease. Nor can you possibly be sharing a domicile with Olive C. Spence.

According to our records, Ms. Spence has been dead since 1911.

Given the above information, I have no choice but to begin an investigation **immediately** into the suspicious activities underway at 43 Old Cemetery Road.

Emphatically,

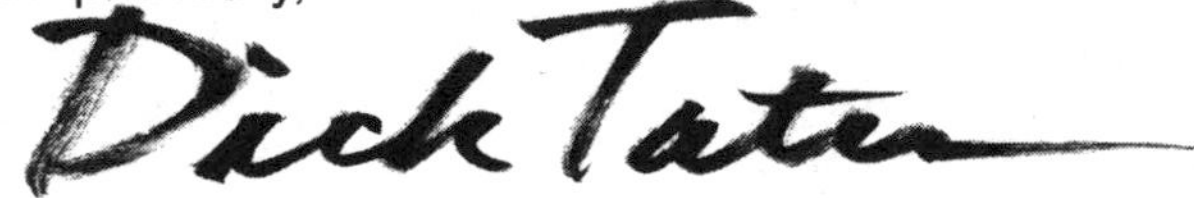

Dick Tater

Friday, September 12
Cliff Hanger, Editor

50 cents
Morning Edition

Local Boy Living in Mansion Without Parents Is "Very Grave Matter"

Dick Tater, director of the International Movement for the Safety & Protection Of Our Kids & Youth (IMSPOOKY), has ordered an investigation into the safety of Seymour Hope, 11.

Tater told *The Ghastly Times* the investigation was prompted by an anonymous letter he received.

"Thanks to a concerned citizen I have learned that a young boy is living in a house without parents," said Tater. "Instead he's living with a man named Ignatius B. Grumply, who is filling this poor child's head with ghost stories and calling it an education."

Grumply does not deny that since June he has lived at 43 Old Cemetery Rd. with Seymour Hope and the ghost of Olive C. Spence.

"It's a lovely arrangement," Grumply told *The Ghastly Times*. "I occupy the second floor of the house. Seymour's bedroom and art studio are located on the third floor. Olive spends much of her time in the cupola, though she likes to float around the rest of the house, too."

When asked to describe a typical day at Spence Mansion, Grumply said: "We meet for meals three times a day in the dining room. Olive usually cooks. Seymour sets the table. I'm in charge of dishwashing. We spend one hour a day, usually after lunch, discussing our book. Other than that, we work independently."

Seymour Hope is living at Spence Mansion without parents.

Tater said his investigation will begin with a visit to Spence Mansion tomorrow. "I plan to get to the bottom of this very grave matter," Tater stated.

IMSPOOKY Director Says Halloween Bad for Children

Bad dreams. Head colds. Cavities.

These are just a few of the side effects associated with Halloween, said Dick Tater, director of the International Movement for the Safety & Protection Of Our Kids & Youth (IMSPOOKY).

"It's time we put an end to this dangerous holiday," Tater said at a press conference yesterday in Washington, D.C.

Tater is expected to make an important announcement about Halloween tonight on

(Continued on page 2, column 1)

IMSPOOKY *(Continued from page 1, column 2)*

Dick Tater discusses the dangers of Halloween.

Tater Tips, the safety news update broadcast weekly on TV and radio.

The IMSPOOKY was established earlier this year by a worldwide committee of concerned parents with children in middle school, often considered the most perilous place for youngsters.

Orders for More Chapters Keep Rolling In

Grumply says new chapters will be ready by Halloween.

In just one month, more than 250,000 readers from around the world have sent money requesting three more chapters of *43 Old Cemetery Road,* a work-in-progress ghost story named for the street address of Spence Mansion.

"The response has been overwhelming," coauthor Ignatius B. Grumply said yesterday. "Olive, Seymour and I are delighted and flattered."

Grumply assured readers that the next three chapters of the book would be ready in six weeks. "Just in time for Halloween," Grumply promised, then jumped for joy.

TATER TIPS

TRANSCRIPT FOR SEPTEMBER 12

DICK TATER: Good evening, and welcome to *Tater Tips*, important safety news from me, your friendly Dick Tater. I'm here tonight with an urgent message.

For the protection of children everywhere, I am canceling Halloween this year and issuing a worldwide ban on all Halloween activities. That includes trick-or-treating, costume parties, bobbing for apples, and especially the telling, writing, and reading of ghost stories.

Ghost stories are bad for children's health. Worse still, ghost stories are a gateway to other dangerous activities and ideas.

As adults, we must protect children from ghost stories and the people who write them.

That's why tomorrow I'm traveling to Ghastly, Illinois, where a man named

Ignatius B. Grumply is living with a young boy and telling him stories about a ghost named Olive C. Spence. Grumply is forcing this child to draw pictures for a book Grumply says he's writing with this ghost.

It's a scam, a hoax, and an outrage! Thank goodness I'm on the case. I'll have more to say about this on the next edition of *Tater Tips*.

Now don't forget: There will be NO Halloween this year. Anyone found wearing a costume, trick-or-treating, bobbing for apples, and/or reading, writing, listening to, or telling a ghost story will be arrested.

Have a safe night. And don't worry about a thing. You can leave the thinking to me, Dick Tater.

VOICEOVER: Tune in next week to *Tater Tips*, brought to you by the International Movement for the Safety & Protection Of Our Kids & Youth.

IGNATIUS B. GRUMPLY

A WRITER IN RESIDENCE

43 OLD CEMETERY ROAD   2ND FLOOR   GHASTLY, ILLINOIS

September 12

Olive C. Spence
The Cupola
43 Old Cemetery Road
Ghastly, Illinois

Dear Olive,

I know it's late, but I think we should have a meeting as soon as practical to discuss the

I'm right here. What do you want to discuss, dear?

Olive! I wish you wouldn't scare me like that. We need a plan for Seymour. I'm afraid this arrangement we have is not entirely legal.

Legal schmeegal. The boy's parents are weasels. They left him in the middle of the night when they slinked off to Europe on their lecture tour. Who knows what would've happened if I weren't still haunting my house—and if you hadn't rented it for the summer?

2.

I agree. But there's a certain Dick Tater at the

Yes, yes. I know. I read his letter, too. You'll just have to go to Washington, D.C., and explain the situation to him.

I'm afraid it's too late for that. He's coming here.

Dick Tater's coming *here*? Without an invitation? Over my dead body!

I didn't think ghosts *had* bodies.

Don't get sassy with me, Iggy.

I'm sorry, Olive. But Mr. Tater has ordered an investigation. Didn't you read today's newspaper?

I was going to. But then I made a pot of tea and forgot where I put my reading glasses. Ugh. My mind is simply mush these days.

You're just a little forgetful sometimes.

As you will be when you're 190 years old.

I'm sure I will. But back to Dick Tater. Some busybody sent him an anonymous letter informing him of our living situation. What should we do?

Tell him Seymour is happy as a lark here.

I will. But what if Mr. Ta

What if nothing, Iggy. We have three chapters to write before Halloween. You'll just have to convince Mr. Tater Tot that we don't need his assistance.

I'll try, Olive. The only probl

Iggy, I haven't got time for this. I must find something to wear for our visitor tomorrow.

Olive, you're invisible to most people, remember? I've seen you only once, and it was just for a split second.

You've had other chances to see me, but you weren't trying hard enough. Besides, I have my pride. I always dress up for company—even if it is a man named Tater. I'll see you tomorrow, dear.

Good night, Olive.

Good night, Iggy.

Ghost Writer in Residence
43 Old Cemetery Road, The Cupola
Ghastly, Illinois

September 12

Dearest Seymour,

I don't know why you're still awake at this hour. But since you are, I want to apologize for something.

I've always assumed you wanted to live here with me. We've been friends since you were born. But for all I know, your feelings might have changed. Now that you're almost grown up, you might prefer to live with relatives or friends—or even try to patch things up with your parents.

There are many options that might be more appealing to an 11-year-old boy than living in an old house with a grumpy writer like Iggy and an ancient ghost like me.

If you want to live somewhere else, you must let me know. This is your life and your decision. I will respect whatever choice you make. And I'm sorry that it didn't occur to me to ask you this before now.

With love and respect,

Olive

SEYMOUR HOPE

Illustrator in Residence

43 Old Cemetery Road
Third Floor
Ghastly, Illinois

September 12

Dear Olive,

Of course I want to live here with you and Mr. Grumply. I don't have any other friends or relatives who are half as cool as you—least of all my crummy parents.

But if you don't want me here anymore, I could run away. Do you want me to?

—Seymour

Ghost Writer in Residence
43 Old Cemetery Road, The Cupola
Ghastly, Illinois

September 12

Dear Seymour,

Run away? Over my dead body!

Seymour, I adore sharing my mansion with you. I just wanted to make sure that's what you want, too.

Now, a man with a silly name will be here tomorrow. Since Iggy and I haven't given you any new chapters to illustrate yet, why don't you sketch our uninvited visitor? His name is Mr. Tater. I'm guessing he'll make an interesting model.

Good night.

Love,

Olive

SEYMOUR HOPE

Illustrator in Residence

43 Old Cemetery Road
Third Floor
Ghastly, Illinois

September 12

Dear Olive,

Will do.

Good night. Rest in peas!

Love,

—Seymour

Ghost Writer in Residence
43 Old Cemetery Road, The Cupola
Ghastly, Illinois

September 12

Dear Seymour,

The expression is "Rest in *peace*."

Now go to bed! It's late. And I want you to be well rested for our visitor tomorrow.

See you in the morning.

Love,

Olive

This is Mr. Tater arriving at 43 Old Cemetery Road.

This is Mr. Grumply trying to explain our publishing company to Mr. Tater.

Sunday, September 14
Cliff Hanger, Editor

$1.50
Morning Edition

Grumply Deranged, Says IMSPOOKY Director; Hope Placed in Ghastly Orphanage

Ignatius B. Grumply was admitted against his will to the Illinois Home for the Deranged yesterday afternoon while Seymour Hope became the newest resident at Ghastly Orphanage.

These surprising developments came after Dick Tater, director of the International Movement for the Safety & Protection Of Our Kids & Youth (IMSPOOKY), visited Grumply and Hope at 43 Old Cemetery Rd.

"I had no idea how disturbed Ignatius Grumply was," said Tater in a press conference yesterday. "Grumply tried to tell me he was homeschooling the boy with the help of a ghost. Far from it! Spence Mansion is neither a home nor a school, but the former residence of a deranged man and the 11-year-old boy he was holding hostage."

Tater said he plans to reunite Hope with his parents as soon as possible.

"Until then," said Tater, "the boy will be safe in Ghastly Orphanage."

Grumply is taken away by state troopers.

Hope will live at local orphanage until his parents return.

Tater Suggests Burning Books on October 31

From coast to coast, towns and schools are busy canceling Halloween parades, costume balls and neighborhood trick-or-treating activities in response to a ban imposed by IMSPOOKY director Dick Tater.

Halloween has long been a favorite holiday in Ghastly, where generations of children have trick-or-treated at Spence Mansion. Legend has it that anyone brave enough to visit Spence Mansion on Halloween receives a mysterious treat from the ghost of Olive C. Spence.

"See?" said Dick Tater, when told of the Ghastly tradition. "That is precisely the kind of unhealthy practice I'm trying to stamp out."

(Continued on page 2, column 1)

GHASTLY ORPHANAGE

New Resident Form

Name of new resident: Seymour Hope

Age: 11

Orphaned ______ Abandoned XX Other ______

Is this child a security risk? Yes ______ No XX

Does this child suffer from physical or mental illness?
Possible mental illness.
Boy claims his best friend is a ghost.

Length of stay: 18th birthday or until his parents claim him

Photo:

This is Mr. Tater not understanding.

This is Mr. Tater making phone calls.

This is Mr. Grumply and me being taken away!

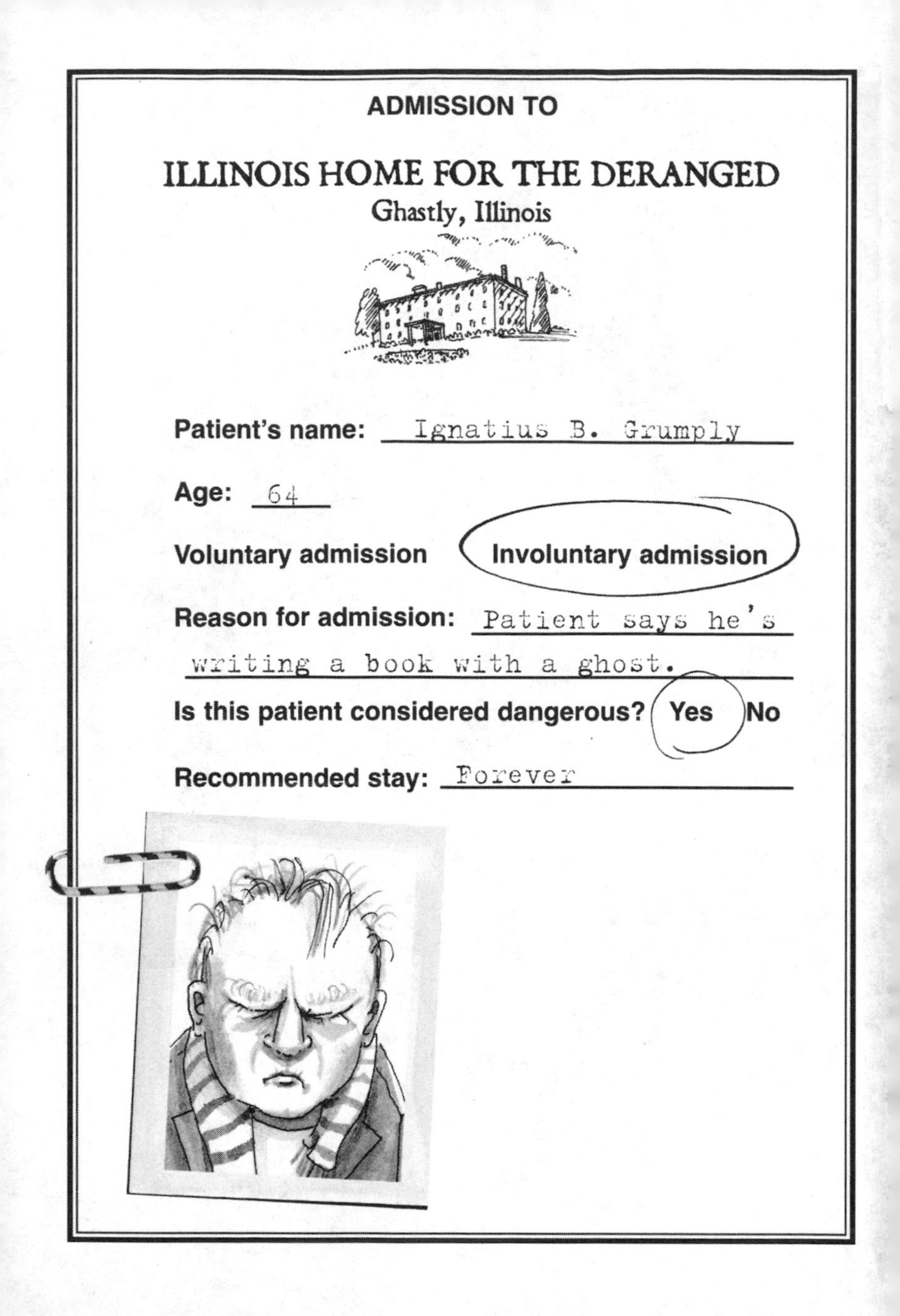

ADMISSION TO

ILLINOIS HOME FOR THE DERANGED

Ghastly, Illinois

Patient's name: Ignatius B. Grumply

Age: 64

Voluntary admission   Involuntary admission

Reason for admission: Patient says he's writing a book with a ghost.

Is this patient considered dangerous? Yes No

Recommended stay: Forever

BOOKS *(Continued from page 1, column 2)*

Dick Tater says bad books make good bonfires.

Tater has suggested a substitute for traditional Halloween activities. "Rather than trick-or-treating, I propose we celebrate October 31 by burning all the ghost stories in the world."

Tater suggests calling the new holiday Dick Tater Appreciation Day.

Was *43 Old Cemetery Road* a Hoax?

Fans of *43 Old Cemetery Road* could be in for a grim disappointment.

Fay Tality admits she fell for scam.

The creators promised to deliver three new chapters of the work in progress to subscribers by October 31. But that hardly seems possible now that coauthor Ignatius B. Grumply is in custody at the Illinois Home for the Deranged and illustrator Seymour Hope is living at Ghastly Orphanage.

Grumply and Hope were collaborating on the book, along with the ghost of Olive C. Spence—or so they claimed.

But according to Dick Tater, director of IMSPOOKY, the project was a clever hoax designed by Grumply to bilk readers out of their dollars and common sense.

"It's embarrassing that we all fell for it," said Fay Tality, president of the Bank of Ghastly. "I guess I liked believing that Olive C. Spence haunted this town. It made Ghastly feel special. But Dick Tater's probably right. Adults should set a good example for children by rejecting silly ghost stories and the people who tell them."

Tality said she plans to burn her entire collection of ghost stories on October 31, as directed by Tater.

"But before I do, I'm going to reread them all," Tality tattled. "Don't tell Dick Tater, but I've always loved scary stories and the people who write them."

INTERNATIONAL MOVEMENT FOR THE SAFETY & PROTECTION OF OUR KIDS & YOUTH

2 BUREAUCRACY AVENUE **WASHINGTON, D.C. 20505**

Dick Tater
Director

INTERNATIONAL EXPRESS MAIL

September 18

Professors Les and Diane Hope
Guests, Hôtel de Sens
1, rue du Figuier
75004 Paris
France

Dear Mr. and Mrs. Hope,

It is my duty to inform you that your son, Seymour Hope, has been removed from the domicile located at 43 Old Cemetery Road and placed in Ghastly Orphanage.

The reason is simple: Ignatius B. Grumply is mentally unstable.

An anonymous letter-writer has assured me that you did not know Grumply was deranged when you agreed to let him care for Seymour in your absence. The same anonymous informant claims that you have been *extremely* busy on your lecture tour, titled "Only Fools (and Children) Believe in Ghosts."

Because I know you share my commitment to protecting children everywhere, I am willing to work with you toward the goal of reuniting you with your son.

Please let me know when you plan to return to Ghastly to reclaim him. I will make every effort to ensure that he is safe, healthy, and eager for the reunion, whenever that may be.

Yours officially,

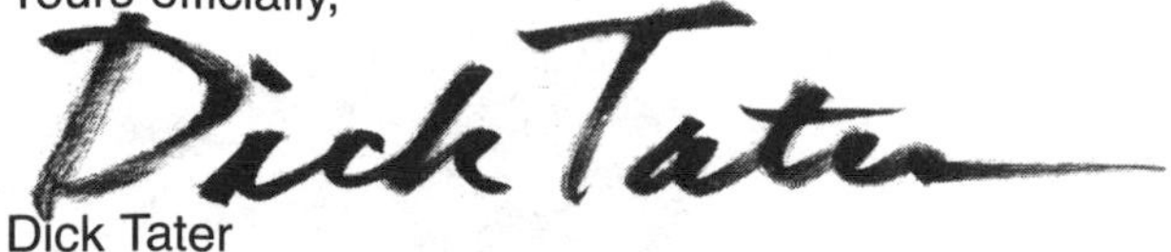

Dick Tater

P.S. If you're wondering how I got your address in France, you can thank the person (or persons) who sent me the anonymous letter.

Hôtel de Sens
1, rue du Figuier
75004 Paris
France

September 19

Dick Tater
Director, IMSPOOKY
2 Bureaucracy Avenue
Washington, D.C. 20505
USA

Dear Mr. Tater,

We hardly know what to say or write—except THANK YOU for protecting our beloved son, Seymour. And thanks, too, to that thoughtful and anonymous letter-writer, whoever he or she (or they) might be.

It's true that we have been extraordinarily busy on our lecture tour. Now we're working on a book titled Only Fools (and Children) Believe in Ghosts:

The Authoritative Anti-Ghost Story. It's the only way we know to convince the millions of children in the world (including our own son) that there are NO such things as ghosts.

We understand this is a particular concern of yours, so we ask for your patience as we finish this important manifesto. We expect to complete our anti-ghost book by the end of next month.

If it's agreeable to you, we will return to Ghastly on October 31 to pick up Seymour. In the meantime, thank you again for keeping our son away from that horrible Mr. Grumply! We had no idea he was a deranged and dangerous madman!

Gratefully yours,

Les & Diane Hope

Les and Diane Hope

P.S. We are enclosing the cover for our new book. Please let us know if you'd like to order a copy.

Only Fools

(and Children)

Believe in Ghosts

Professors Les and Diane Hope

"Sure to be a bestseller!" —L.H. and D.H.

INTERNATIONAL MOVEMENT FOR THE SAFETY & PROTECTION OF OUR KIDS & YOUTH

2 BUREAUCRACY AVENUE **WASHINGTON, D.C. 20505**

Dick Tater
Director

September 24

Professors Les and Diane Hope
Guests, Hôtel de Sens
1, rue du Figuier
75004 Paris
France

Dear Mr. and Mrs. Hope,

Thank you for your prompt response. Your new book is *exactly* what children today need.

I would like to order five million copies. My intention is to replace every ghost story on every bookshelf with *Only Fools (and Children) Believe in Ghosts: The Authoritative Anti-Ghost Story*.

Please don't worry about Seymour. He will be safe at Ghastly Orphanage until you return on October 31.

And don't worry about Ignatius B. Grumply, either. Patients at the Illinois Home for the Deranged are kept in solitary confinement. Rest assured that Ignatius B. Grumply is no longer a threat to children or society.

Authoritatively yours,

Dick Tater

Dick Tater

ILLINOIS HOME FOR THE DERANGED

PATIENT REQUEST FORM

NAME OF PATIENT: Ignatius B. Grumply

ITEM(S) REQUESTED: Paper, Pens,
Envelopes, Stamps

REASON: Patient says he will become a danger to himself and others if he is unable to write.

APPROVED
SEPT. 27

ILLINOIS HOME FOR THE DERANGED

September 28

1 Cuckoo Lane
Ghastly, Illinois

Olive C. Spence
The Cupola
43 Old Cemetery Road
Ghastly, Illinois

Dear Olive,

Of all the insufferable indignities I've been subjected to in my life, *this* takes the cake.

Just because I mentioned to Mr. Tater that I'd fallen in love with a talented and glamorous writer who happens to be a ghost, I'm locked up in a home for the *deranged*. It's outrageous, and I have every intention of bringing legal action against that petty little Dick Tater—just as soon as I figure out a way to escape.

But enough about me. I'm sick with worry about Seymour. Tater refused to tell me where he was taking him. Do you know? If so, please write back and assure me that Seymour's all right. I worry what might become of that poor child if Tater has anything to say in the matter.

And what about you, Olive? Are you well? Are you still at Spence Mansion? I miss you madly.

Please write back as soon as humanly—or ghostly—possible.

Hopelessly devoted,

Ignatius

Ignatius

GHASTLY ORPHANAGE

66 Gruel Drive
Ghastly, Illinois

September 29

Olive C. Spence
The Cupola
43 Old Cemetery Road
Ghastly, Illinois

Dear Olive,

I finally found some paper so I could write you a letter. I can't believe I didn't even get to say good-bye to you or Shadow.

Dick Tater said there was no competent or legal guardian to take care of me at 43 Old Cemetery Road. The more Mr. Grumply tried to explain it, the worse it got. Were you there? Did you see what happened? Is Mr. Grumply in jail? Is it illegal for us to live together and work on our book?

I hate living here. I've drawn some pictures so you can see for yourself how lousy this place is.

Love,

—Seymour

The place looks creepy from the outside.

But it's even worse inside.

This is where they feed us.

The food is terrible.

Classroom
This is where we go to school.
We have to wear uniforms!
Dormitory
This is where I sleep.
My bed is lumpy.
BOOKS!
At least the bookmobile comes once a week.

Ghost Writer in Residence
43 Old Cemetery Road, The Cupola
Ghastly, Illinois

September 30

Ignatius B. Grumply
Patient, Illinois Home for the Deranged
1 Cuckoo Lane
Ghastly, Illinois

Seymour Hope
Resident, Ghastly Orphanage
66 Gruel Drive
Ghastly, Illinois

Dear Iggy and Seymour,

Oh, darlings! I saw the whole shameful showdown with Mr. Tater Tot. I'm sorry that I wasn't able to be more helpful to you in your hour of need. I was foolishly wearing high-heeled boots that were stylish but not

very practical in a crisis—
especially since I haven't
worn heels in 110 years.
Forgiveness, please.

At least now I know
where you are. (You can
see from the addresses
listed on the previous
page where the other is.)
It's all very worrisome,
and I'm afraid the news
here is no better.

Early this morning, I floated over to the Ghastly Gourmand for tea. I was too distracted to brew my own. While there, I couldn't help overhear the locals discussing . . . us!

Kay Daver said: "There's no way on earth they can continue publishing their book now that Grumply's in the nut house and the poor kid's in the orphanage. Olive can't write the whole thing on her own." To which Fay Tality replied: "Didn't you see Dick Tater on TV the other night? There's no ghost in that mansion. It's a joke. The book was just a scam by Grumply." To which Mac Awbrah added: "Fay's right. It was all a cheap trick." To which Shirley U. Jest said: "I'm canceling my order for the next three chapters of *43 Old Cemetery Road*. I want my money back!" To which they all said in unison: "Me, too!"

Well, of course by that point I had completely lost my appetite for tea, and returned home.

But do you see the problem, boys? Our readers are turning against us. They think we're a joke. A trick! They don't take us the least bit seriously. If our readers all demand refunds, we'll have to sell the house—and then what? Where will we live? What will we do?

We've simply *got* to deliver the next three chapters of our book by Halloween. But how can we do so under our current circumstances? Do either of you have an idea on how we should proceed—other than with caution?

Yours in spirit,

Olive

P.S. Shadow misses you both desperately, but is otherwise fine.

GHASTLY ORPHANAGE

66 Gruel Drive
Ghastly, Illinois

October 1

Ignatius B. Grumply
Patient, Illinois Home for the Deranged
1 Cuckoo Lane
Ghastly, Illinois

Dear Mr. Grumply,

Sorry to hear you're in the asylum. I bet you're already planning your escape. When you're free, can you come get me? Thanks.

I have an idea for the next three chapters of our book. Remember all those mysteries Olive told us she wrote during her life? The ones she could never get anyone to publish? What if she found one of those

2.

stories and made copies of it for our customers? She could enclose a letter with the story explaining to readers that she's sending them a special mystery for Halloween. Then, when we're all home again, we can get back to work on *43 Old Cemetery Road.*

I think people would love to read one of Olive's stories. She's a LEGEND in this town!

If you like this idea, please write to Olive. I get only two stamps every other week.

Miss you lots. Don't forget to come rescue me!

ILLINOIS HOME FOR THE DERANGED

1 Cuckoo Lane
Ghastly, Illinois

October 2

Olive C. Spence
The Cupola
43 Old Cemetery Road
Ghastly, Illinois

Dear Olive,

Seymour has a brilliant idea. (See enclosed letter.)

I'd love to read your old manuscripts, too. But I'd prefer to do so in the comfort of my own reading chair.

Olive, if you'll work on satisfying our customers, I'll devise escape plans for Seymour and me. We'll be back in business at 43 Old Cemetery Road in no time.

Please forward this letter to Seymour, as I haven't the energy to copy it. I hope the food is better where you are, Seymour. On the upside, I seem to be losing a few unwanted pounds.

Till very soon, I hope.

Love,

Ignatius

Ignatius

Ghost Writer in Residence
43 Old Cemetery Road, The Cupola
Ghastly, Illinois

October 3

Ignatius B. Grumply
Patient, Illinois Home for the Deranged
1 Cuckoo Lane
Ghastly, Illinois

Seymour Hope
Resident, Ghastly Orphanage
66 Gruel Drive
Ghastly, Illinois

Dear Iggy and Seymour,

It's agreed! And I can promise our customers that more chapters of *43 Old Cemetery Road* will be forthcoming when the three of us are reunited.

While I do that, Iggy will escape his handlers and then retrieve Seymour from the orphanage. Also, Iggy, please figure out a way to make our living arrangement legal.

Darling Seymour, may I ask that you continue sketching while you wait for Iggy? Artists must keep their fingers and minds nimble—even in times of adversity.

We have a frightening amount of work ahead of us!

Yours in sensible shoes,

Olive

P.S. I do hope I can find my old manuscripts. I haven't seen them since my death almost a century ago.

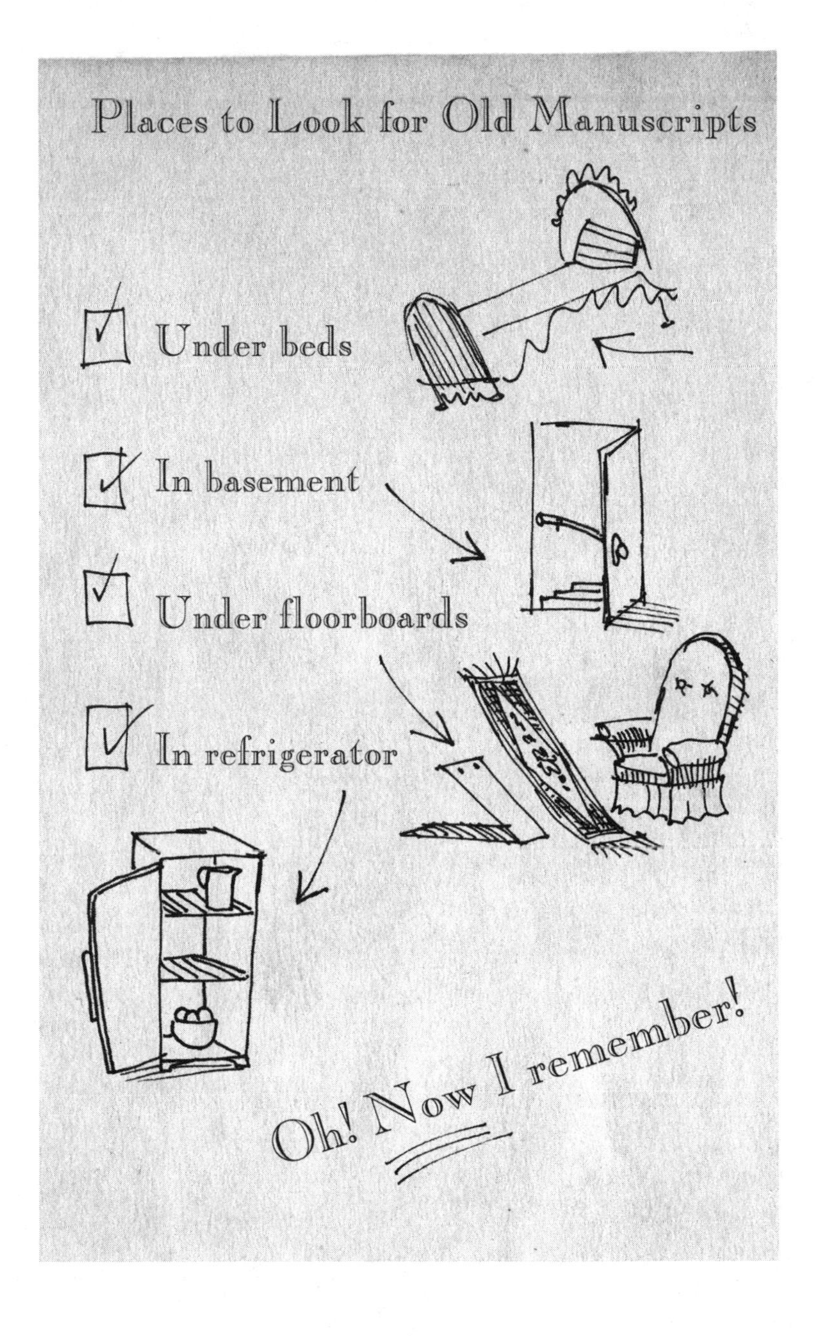
Places to Look for Old Manuscripts
Under beds
In basement
Under floorboards
In refrigerator
Oh! Now I remember!

Ghost Writer in Residence
43 Old Cemetery Road, The Cupola
Ghastly, Illinois

October 4

Ms. Fay Tality
President, Bank of Ghastly
6 Scary Street
Ghastly, Illinois

Dear Ms. Tality,

I couldn't help overhearing you recently at the Ghastly Gourmand. It's a shame you've begun doubting my existence. I was a dear friend of your great-grandfather, who established the Bank of Ghastly in 1904. In fact, I was one of his first customers.

I'm writing to you because I'm in a bit of a pickle. I'm desperately trying to locate my old manuscripts. These were the stories I tried for years to get published and couldn't. My problem is this: I can't for the life—or death—of me remember where I've stored them. But I have a strong hunch they might be in my safe-deposit box at your bank.

I am enclosing my box key. Your great-grandfather was kind enough to give me box 0. Will you please open the box with this key and send me the contents?

I realize that I am probably asking you to violate a bank rule or two. But I hope that you'll agree to do this small favor for me in exchange for all the Halloween treats I left out for you over the years. I watched you every year from my cupola. I especially enjoyed the year you dressed as a pirate. You looked just like your great-grandfather!

With fingers crossed,

Olive C. Spence

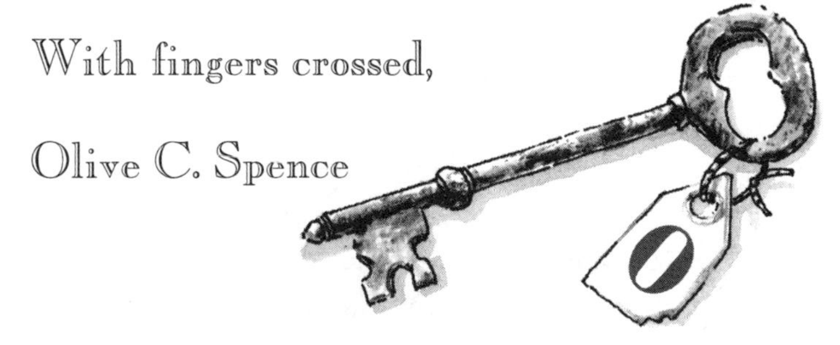

BANK OF GHASTLY
6 SCARY STREET
GHASTLY, ILLINOIS

Fay Tality
President

October 6

Wise Guy/Gal
43 Old Cemetery Road
Ghastly, Illinois

Dear Wise Guy or Gal,

Look here, I don't know what kind of joke you're playing, but I'll have you know that I don't believe in ghosts—not anymore, anyway.

Of course as a child I believed in ghosts—or *a* ghost, I should say. Back then everyone in Ghastly believed that Olive C. Spence haunted her old house. And yes, I *did* trick-or-treat one Halloween at Spence Mansion dressed as a pirate. I have no idea how you know this, but it's hardly proof that *you're* the ghost of Olive C. Spence.

I'm assuming your letter has something to do with the hateful little trick Mr. Grumply is playing on our town. Well, you'll not fool me! I plan to burn the first three chapters of "your" book, just as Mr. Tater said we should.

It might interest you to know that I opened safe-deposit box 0—just to satisfy my own curiosity. That box has been something of a mystery to me since the day I started working here 40 years ago.

Of course there were no manuscripts hidden inside the box. The only thing I found was another key—this one considerably rusty—which I am keeping front and center on my desk until I can get to the bottom of this matter.

In the meantime, I am returning your safe-deposit key to you. I hope this will put an end to your silly pranks.

Yours with interest compounded over time,

Fay Tality

P.S. Not that it matters, but since we're on the topic, I will confess that some of my fondest childhood memories are of Halloweens spent trying to muster the courage to walk up the porch steps at 43 Old Cemetery Road. If Dick Tater hadn't canceled Halloween, I'd be tempted to stop by that old house on October 31—just for old times' sake.

P.P.S. Remember the year you gave out licorice jump ropes to all the trick-or-treaters who came to your door? Of course you don't remember, because you don't *exist!*

P.P.P.S. Or do you? And now where is that rusty key I placed on my desk? It was here just a moment ago! This is all very troubling. Please do not write to me again.

Ghost Writer in Residence
43 Old Cemetery Road, The Cupola
Ghastly, Illinois

October 7

Mr. Ike N. Openitt
Owner, Ghastly Lock & Key
18 Scary Street
Ghastly, Illinois

Dear Mr. Openitt,

I have recently come into possession of an antique key. The problem is, I can't remember what it unlocks. I only know that my most valuable papers are locked behind the door that can be opened with this key.

Will you please examine the key and tell me what kind of door it fits? I will be happy to pay for your time and trouble.

This is not a joke or a prank. If you don't believe me, I will tell your sister about the time you picked the lock to her diary.

Yours in spirit,

Olive C. Spence

Ghastly Lock & Key
18 Scary Street
Ghastly, Illinois

Ike N. Openitt
Locksmith

October 8

Somebody Who's Living at
43 Old Cemetery Road
Ghastly, Illinois

Dear Somebody,

I've got half a mind to forward this letter straight to the police. But then they'd want to know if I really picked the lock to my sister's diary 35 years ago. And I don't really want to get into all that, if you know what I'm saying.

Now, about that rusty key you sent: It isn't a door key. Looks more like a key to an old trunk. Make that a *really* old trunk.

If I were you, I'd ask Mac Awbrah over at Ghastly Antiques to have a look at it. But how could I be you if *you* aren't even you? Now I've got a headache.

I'm returning your key with my invoice.

Sincerely,

Ike N. Openitt

Ike N. Openitt

INVOICE **1807**

Ghastly Lock & Key
18 Scary Street
Ghastly, Illinois

DATE: October 8

SERVICE:	FEE:
Key examination	

No charge. Just <u>don't</u> talk to my sister.

Ghost Writer in Residence
43 Old Cemetery Road, The Cupola
Ghastly, Illinois

October 9

Mac Awbrah
Owner, Ghastly Antiques
2 Scary Street
Ghastly, Illinois

Dear Mr. Awbrah,

Do you happen to have an old trunk that can be opened with the enclosed key?

Please respond with alacrity, as some of my most valuable possessions are at stake.

I know over the years you've taken a strange delight in refuting the fact that I haunt Ghastly—despite my frequent

2.

appearances in that lovely etched mirror in your shop. If I must take stronger measures to convince you of my existence, I shall.

Yours in spirit,

Olive C. Spence

O.C.S.

43 Old Cemetery Road, The Cupola

Ghastly, Illinois

October 10

Whoever Is Posing as Olive C. Spence
43 Old Cemetery Road
Ghastly, Illinois

Dear Whoever You Are,

I don't know who you are, but I don't like people who waste my time. And I especially don't like being threatened.

But I do like antiques. And if you must know, the key you sent is from the Victorian era. If I had to guess, I'd say it came out of Spence Mansion. It probably opens an old trunk somewhere in the house.

Have you asked Les and Diane Hope about this key? If you're really Olive C. Spence, you'd know that the Hopes sold a lot of things from your house when they bought

2.

it 12 years ago. It's possible they sold the trunk you're looking for. Or maybe they took it with them to France. Just a guess.

I am returning your key with this letter. Now, if you will excuse me, an unusual chill has descended upon my shop. I must find my sweater.

Mac Awbrah

Mac Awbrah

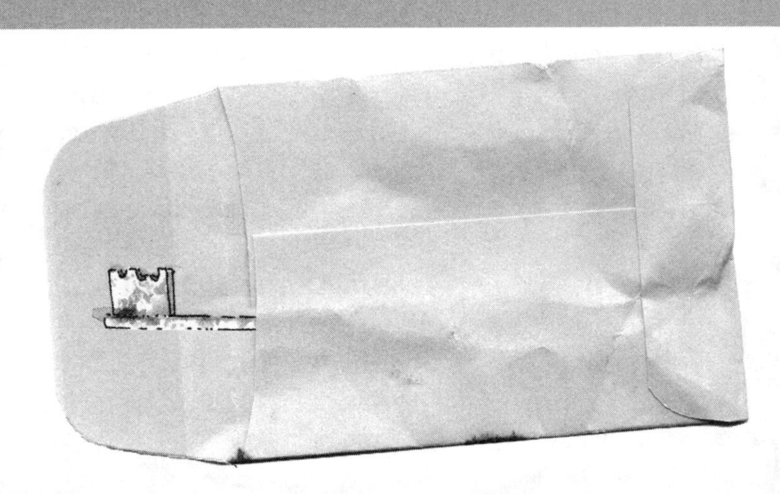

O.C.S.
43 Old Cemetery Road
Ghastly, Illinois
U.S.A.
GHASTLY
AM
Oct 11
IL
READ
BANNED
BOOKS
URGENT
Professors Les and Diane Hope
Guests, Hôtel de Sens
1, rue du Figuier
75004 Paris
France
INTERNATIONAL
EXPRESS MAIL

Ghost Writer in Residence
43 Old Cemetery Road, The Cupola
Ghastly, Illinois

October 11

Professors Les and Diane Hope
Guests, Hôtel de Sens
1, rue du Figuier
75004 Paris
France

You scoundrels.

Until now I've never cared to have any contact with you. But I have a sneaking suspicion you stole from my house a trunk containing priceless manuscripts.

I want the trunk and all of its contents back immediately.

I am making arrangements with my

colleagues in the ghost network to transport my belongings from Paris to Ghastly. All I ask is that you leave the trunk in the lobby of your hotel. My contacts will take it from there.

Grimly,

Olive C. Spence

P.S. For your information, Seymour, the son you so heartlessly abandoned in May, is perfectly happy without you. Or rather, he *will* be—as soon as Ignatius Grumply retrieves him from Ghastly Orphanage.

Hôtel de Sens
1, rue du Figuier
75004 Paris
France

October 14

Seymour Hope
43 Old Cemetery Road
Ghastly, Illinois USA

PAR AVION

Dear Seymour,

Still playing your little ghost games, are you?

Look, kid. We don't know how you escaped from that orphanage, but if you think you can sabotage our careers again, forget it. Our new book, *Only Fools (and Children) Believe in Ghosts: The Authoritative Anti-Ghost Story*, is almost done. And we've already sold five million copies to Dick Tater!

We're coming back to Ghastly on October 31 to get your sorry little self. Then we're going on a book tour—as a family—and you're going to tell the whole world about your ghost friend, Olive. Why? Because then you'll prove our thesis that only fools and children (and in your case, foolish children) believe in ghosts.

And if you refuse to cooperate? Well, let's just say there are orphanages all over the world that have room for one more little brat like you.

See you soon, kid. Oh, and you can forget about Grumply saving your hide. The geezer's in the loony bin—where he belongs.

Mom + Dad

Ghost Writer in Residence
43 Old Cemetery Road, The Cupola
Ghastly, Illinois

October 20

Professors Les and Diane Hope
Guests, Hôtel de Sens
1, rue du Figuier
75004 Paris
France

Miserable miscreants,

You are truly repellent human beings and deplorable parents. In my younger days, I kept a goodly supply of itching powder on my desk to sprinkle in letters like this. But because I have misplaced my itching powder as well as my manuscripts, my only comfort is knowing that one day you will get exactly what you deserve. Wretched people always do.

Also, I can assure you that Ignatius Grumply is one of the sanest and most capable men I have ever had the pleasure of knowing. By the time you read these words, he and Seymour will almost certainly be back here at Spence Mansion, where they belong.

Confidently,

Olive C. Spence

ILLINOIS HOME FOR THE DERANGED

October 21

1 Cuckoo Lane
Ghastly, Illinois

Seymour Hope
Resident, Ghastly Orphanage
66 Gruel Drive
Ghastly, Illinois

Dear Seymour,

I'd hoped to have flown this cuckoo's nest by now so that I could come rescue you from your captors. I'm sorry to report that escaping is turning out to be more difficult than I'd imagined.

My only contact here is the patient in the next cell. I thought he might be willing to share escape strategies that have worked in the past. So I devised an alphabet of knocks for us to communicate. One knock equals "a," two knocks equal "b," and so forth.

It's working fine, but it's a rare day when we're able to exchange more than a few words. So far my cell neighbor has told me that someone escaped from this miserable place several years ago in the middle of the night using a clever strategy that employed . . .

Well, that's as far as we've gotten.

Please don't give up on me, Seymour. I miss you more than words can express.

Love, and as we say here,

2 knocks 25 knocks 5 knocks-2 knocks 25 knocks 5 knocks!

Ignatius

Ignatius

Ghastly Orphanage
66

Since its founding in 1885, Ghastly Orphanage has provided a home for orphaned and abandoned children.

Mr. Grumply,

I would never give up on you!

12-15-22-5,

—Seymour

POST CARD

USA READ

GHASTLY • IL • PM Oct 22

Ignatius B. Grumply
Patient
Illinois Home for the Deranged
1 Cuckoo Lane
Ghastly, Illinois

Hi, Olive!

I'm still sketching, like you told me to do. But I'm getting worried about Mr. Grumply. In his last letter, he sounded so lonely and sad.

Hope you're doing okay. Please send news—good or bad. Can you also send me some stamps?

Love,

—Seymour

P.S. Tell Shadow I said HI.

Olive C. Spence
The Cupola
43 Old Cemetery Road
Ghastly, Illinois

Ghost Writer in Residence
43 Old Cemetery Road, The Cupola
Ghastly, Illinois

October 23

Seymour Hope
Resident, Ghastly Orphanage
66 Gruel Drive
Ghastly, Illinois

Dearest Seymour,

I have so much to tell you! I shan't waste time or paper with flowery openings, because I trust you know how much I miss you.

First the good news: I know where my old manuscripts are! They're in a trunk. I even have the key.

The bad news is, I don't know where the blasted trunk is. I've looked everywhere on earth.

I'm so sorry, dear. Our deadline is just eight

days away. I've failed miserably in my only assignment. I don't know what to do—except tremble with rage whenever I hear that meddlesome Dick Tater. None of this would've happened if he weren't such a wretched man.

Now I'm getting myself all worked up. I'll write again when I'm in a better mood and have more hopeful news to share.

Almost forgot your stamps! Here they are.

Please think of a way to rescue Iggy from the asylum. I'm afraid Dick Tater had him committed for life. Stupid man! I'm tempted to pay that ridiculous potato head a visit. I think I shall!

Immortal love,

Olive

TATER TIPS

TRANSCRIPT FOR OCTOBER 24

DICK TATER: Good evening, and welcome to *Tater Tips,* important safety news from me, your friendly Dick Tater. I'm here tonight to remind you that there will be no Halloween this year. Instead, we'll celebrate October 31 with Dick Tater Appreciation Day, when we'll burn all of the ghost stories in the world. I invite everyone listening tonight to round up your dangerous books and take them to your local library or bookmobile. Earlier today I ordered librarians everywhere to prepare giant bonfires so that we can

Oh, for pity's sake.

I . . . I . . . (ahem) Forgive me, viewers. I seem to have lost my place in the *Tater Tips* script. As I was saying, I

You, sir, are a fool.

What's happening here? I'm trying

to read my *Tater Tips* script.

What makes you think you have the right to tell people what they can and cannot read?

This is a live broadcast. Who are you? Where is this coming from? If someone has broken into the secret IMSPOOKY TV studio, there will be a stiff penalty, I can assure you! We have armed guards on duty at every door to prevent trespassers!

I don't need doors. I'm a ghost from Ghastly, Illinois. I can travel through the airwaves if I so choose.

Oh, so that's what this is all about: the legend of Ghastly. Well, that little myth has gone on long enough. I'm putting an end to all that because I am

A bore.

Who is this? I demand to know!

I'm Olive C. Spence.

You are not! Olive C. Spence is dead. She died in 1911.

Yes, but I had unfinished business.

No one is allowed to interrupt my *Tater Tips* broadcast—especially not ghosts.

Normally I don't interrupt. Or at least I try not to. But I have a book to write, Mr. Tater Tot, and I need my coauthor and illustrator to help me. Now listen closely. I will give you ten minutes to release Ignatius Grumply from the Illinois Home for the Deranged and Seymour Hope from Ghastly Orphanage.

This is some kind of trick or black magic. Ghosts don't exist!

Why do you insist on telling people I don't exist? I don't tell people you don't exist—even though there are moments I wish you didn't.

4.

You are a very dangerous person, whoever you are. And I intend to expose you as the safety threat you are.

Blah blah blah.

I will get to the bottom of this, even if it requires an exhumation.

Over my dead body.

Exactly!

Tater Plans to Exhume Spence's Body:

"Give up the ghost, Ghastly," says Tater

In an effort to put to rest rumors that the ghost of Olive C. Spence is haunting Ghastly, the director of the International Movement for the Safety & Protection Of Our Kids & Youth (IMSPOOKY) announced plans to exhume Spence's body next week.

"It's time to give up the ghost, Ghastly," Tater said in an emergency press conference held last night.

Tater said he plans to dig up Spence's coffin and put the open casket on display. "That way, everyone can see with their own eyes that this woman is dead and gone," Tater explained.

Spence died in 1911. Her obituary is reprinted below.

Tater ended the press conference by apologizing for his odd performance on *Tater Tips* last night, in which he appeared to be engaged in a heated debate with an unseen opponent.

"I've been working around the clock preparing for Dick Tater Appreciation Day," said Tater, who blamed his bizarre behavior on lack of sleep.

Tater will dig up Spence's coffin on Wednesday.

Olive C. Spence Is Dead; Ghastly's Original Free Spirit Passes Away

No funeral is planned for Spence.

Olive C. Spence, 93, died last night in the home she built on Old Cemetery Road.

Sources say the cause of Spence's death was a heart broken by publishers' continued rejection of her books.

Shortly before her death, Spence vowed to haunt her house and hometown until one of her manuscripts was published. "I shall either publish or never truly perish," Spence told this newspaper last year.

No funeral service is planned for Spence, who left specific instructions for the burial with Kerry N. Barry at Barry Bros. Funeral Parlor.

Page 2 **THE GHASTLY TIMES** October 25

Balm Refuses to Cooperate in Book Burning

"Over my dead body!"

That's how M. Balm described his reaction to news that he must use the Ghastly bookmobile to collect all the ghost stories in town for a mandatory book burning on October 31.

"I will go to my grave defending a person's right to read ghost stories and other so-called bad books," said Balm. "Mr. Tater thinks they're dangerous. But to my mind, there's nothing more dangerous than a person who tries to dictate what books people can read. It's as offensive as telling people what they can think!"

M. Balm defends the right to read ghost stories.

Readers Demand Refunds

Readers who sent $3 to Spence Mansion, located at 43 Old Cemetery Rd., are now sending requests for refunds to the same address.

"If we're not going to get more chapters of the book, we deserve to get our money back," said Shirley U. Jest, owner of the Ghastly Gourmand and a subscriber to the ghost story in progress.

"Of course I don't know who's going to send us a refund now," Jest continued. "Shadow, Seymour's cat, is the only one left at the house. Well, Shadow and the ghost of Olive C. Spence, if you believe in ghosts."

Jest said she plans to burn the first three chapters of *43 Old Cemetery Road* on October 31.

Jest says readers have right to refund.

"It's the law, so we have to do it," Jest said. "But I'm going to reread the first three chapters before I burn them. Don't tell Dick Tater, but I really do love ghost stories."

GHASTLY ORPHANAGE

66 Gruel Drive
Ghastly, Illinois

October 25

Olive C. Spence
The Cupola
43 Old Cemetery Road
Ghastly, Illinois

Dear Olive,

I just got your letter. Don't worry! I'll help you look for your old manuscripts. I've thought of an escape plan.

The bookmobile from the Ghastly Public Library comes here every Wednesday afternoon. If you can board the bookmobile in the morning before Mr. Balm leaves the library, I'll hide in it when he gets here. Together, we'll take the bookmobile to the Illinois Home for the Deranged, where we'll rescue Mr. Grumply.

What do you think?

Love,

—Seymour

Ghost Writer in Residence
43 Old Cemetery Road, The Cupola
Ghastly, Illinois

October 27

Seymour Hope
Resident, Ghastly Orphanage
66 Gruel Drive
Ghastly, Illinois

Dear Seymour,

I think it's the perfect plan. You deserve a medal for cleverness!

I'm sure M. Balm won't mind if we borrow his bookmobile for just a little while. We'll make it up to him somehow.

I'll meet you in the bookmobile. Can you bring a sketchpad and pencil? Iggy will want to see how we pulled this one off.

2.

There are some grave developments here at home, dear. I'll explain in more detail when I see you.

Forever yours,

Olive

This is the bookmobile arriving at Ghastly Orphanage.

This is Olive and me in the bookmobile.

This is Olive driving the bookmobile.

This is M. Balm freaking out.

This is us arriving at the Illinois Home for the Deranged.

ILLINOIS HOME FOR THE DERANGED

1 Cuckoo Lane
Ghastly, Illinois

October 29

Olive C. Spence
The Cupola
43 Old Cemetery Road
Ghastly, Illinois

My darling Olive (or as I've grown accustomed to thinking: 13-25 4-1-18-12-9-14-7 15-12-9-22-5),

Your silence suggests that you've lost faith in me. I don't blame you. I promised to escape from this hideous place weeks ago so that I could rescue Seymour. Meanwhile, here I sit, counting out letters on my fingers, knocking on walls, and slowly going craz

Hello, darling.

Olive! You frightened me. Is that really you?

Of course it's me. And Seymour's waiting out in the bookmobile with M. Balm.

Bookmobile? Is Seymour all right? Are you okay?

Calm down, darling. I'll explain everything later. We have to hurry home. Mr. Tater is making preparations to have my body exhumed tonight.

Exhumed?

Yes, dear. Now follow my glasses. We're breaking out of here.

TATER TIPS

TRANSCRIPT FOR OCTOBER 29

DICK TATER: Good evening, and welcome to *Tater Tips,* important safety news from me, your friendly Dick Tater. Tonight we're broadcasting live from the gravesite of Olive C. Spence in Ghastly, Illinois. I have a crew hard at work, digging up one of Ghastly's oldest and cruelest jokes. That's right. I'm talking about the legend of Olive C. Spence, the woman who is believed by many to haunt her old house and town. How are we doing, boys?

UNNAMED DIGGER #1: Almost there, boss.

DICK TATER: Good. Because I want to show all the people watching *Tater Tips* tonight the truth, which isn't always pretty. In fact, folks, I should warn you that what we're about to see will be shocking to behold. When we open Spence's coffin, we're going to find a woman who died 97 years ago. Who can predict what the ravages of time and nature have done to her body?

UNNAMED DIGGER #2: We're bringing her up, boss.

[Enter Ignatius Grumply and Seymour Hope]

IGNATIUS GRUMPLY: How dare you dig up Olive's coffin!

DICK TATER: What are you doing here? You're supposed to be in the nut house.

SEYMOUR HOPE: He escaped, just like I did.

DICK TATER: Why you little . . . but perhaps it's for the best. This might be exactly the shock therapy you need, young man, to set your mind straight about ghosts and other such nonsense. Open the coffin, boys!

UNNAMED DIGGER #3: Uh, we can't, sir. It's locked.

Oh, I just remembered something!

DICK TATER: I don't care if it is locked. Open it!

UNNAMED DIGGER #1: Wait. Something's happening with the lock.

Of course something's happening, you mule. I'm using my key to unlock my coffin.

UNNAMED DIGGER #2: Will ya look at that? A rusty old key is opening the coffin. And look what's inside.

SEYMOUR HOPE: Olive! Your manuscripts!

IGNATIUS GRUMPLY: You hid them in your coffin! Brilliant!

Thank you, dear. I only wish I'd remembered before now.

DICK TATER: What is the meaning of this? I demand an explanation. How did-who did-hee-hee-hee!

[Tater begins jumping around and scratching himself uncontrollably]

UNNAMED DIGGER #3: You okay, boss?

DICK TATER *[continues frenetic jumping and scratching]*: Haw, hee, ho-ho-ho! Hee-hee, haw-haw, ho!

UNNAMED DIGGER #1: Um, boss?

DICK TATER: Hiya, waa-waa! Hiya-hiya, ho-ho-ho!

IGNATIUS GRUMPLY *[laughing]*: Olive, what on earth are you doing to him?

I found my stash of itching powder in my coffin, too. I knew I put it somewhere! I just sprinkled a little down Mr. Tater's pants.

DICK TATER *[more jumping and scratching]*: Hi-ho, hee-hee-hee, gimme gummy goomy! Gimme goomy gummy gummy!

[Sound of sirens in distance]

Thursday, October 30
Cliff Hanger, Editor

"Your Secrets Are Our Business"

50 cents
Morning Edition

Grave Surprise!

Tater taken away after bizarre outburst

Spence's coffin contains her unpublished works.

It was a scene straight out of the movies.

Last night as onlookers gasped at the discovery of unpublished manuscripts in the coffin of Olive C. Spence, Dick Tater was taken away in a straitjacket to the Illinois Home for the Deranged.

Tater, director of the International Movement for the Safety & Protection Of Our Kids & Youth (IMSPOOKY), reportedly suffered a nervous breakdown due to the stress of the Spence exhumation and the long hours devoted to abolishing Halloween.

The discovery of Spence's manuscripts in her coffin prompted funeral director Kerry N. Barry IV, the great-grandson of the founder of Barry Bros. Funeral Parlor, to do a little digging of his own.

"I found the instructions Miss Spence left for my great-grandfather," Barry told *The Ghastly Times*. "She wrote him a letter shortly before her death and told him she wanted all of her manuscripts buried in the coffin."

But what about her body?

"I'm not sure what became of that," Barry said with a shrug. "And I'm not sure I want to know. There's no evidence Miss Spence spent any time at all in that coffin."

Grumply and Hope Reunited—for Now

Grumply and Hope return to Spence Mansion.

Ignatius B. Grumply and Seymour Hope have returned to 43 Old Cemetery Rd. to live together—for now, anyway.

The 64-year-old author and the 11-year-old illustrator escaped yesterday from the Illinois Home for the Deranged and Ghastly Orphanage, respectively. It is unclear whether Grumply and Hope are still considered wards of the state.

The Ghastly Times has learned that Professors Les and Diane Hope are scheduled to arrive in Ghastly tomorrow to pick up their son. The couple has been in Europe working on their book.

Balm the Opposite of Calm

M. Balm, chief librarian at the Ghastly Public Library, is recovering from a high-speed bookmobile ride yesterday that nearly claimed his life.

According to Balm, he and Seymour Hope were transported by an invisible driver from Ghastly Orphanage to the Illinois Home for the Deranged, where Ignatius B. Grumply joined them.

"Then the three of us were driven to Spence Mansion at 150 miles an hour by a phantom driver who almost killed us," said Balm.

Balm refused to speculate whether the bookmobile is haunted.

"If you're asking whether or not I believe in ghosts, the answer is I don't know," said Balm. "All I know is I believe in the right to read ghost stories."

Last week Balm promised to go to his grave defending the right to read ghost stories.

"And it looks like I almost just did," added Balm.

M. Balm says bookmobile ride nearly killed him.

IGNATIUS B. GRUMPLY

A WRITER IN RESIDENCE

43 OLD CEMETERY ROAD 2ND FLOOR GHASTLY, ILLINOIS

October 30

Olive C. Spence
The Cupola
43 Old Cemetery Road
Ghastly, Illinois

Dear Olive,

Thank goodness you found your manuscripts. Now we have something to send our readers. Please choose one story for us to publish. I'll ask Seymour to begi

I'm afraid I have some bad news.

Olive! How many times do I have to ask you not to sneak up on me like that?

Sorry, dear. But I really do have some unfortunate news.

You lost your manuscripts again?

No, I have them. I reread them all last night.

So what's the bad news?

They're not the least bit frightening.

Your manuscripts? Olive, I don't believe you.

Oh, they're perfectly fine as far as mysteries go. But a ghost story should be scary, don't you think? And what we've been through these past two months with Dick Tater is much more frightening than anything I could possibly make up. What do you say we publish *that* story instead?

I say you're brilliant, as always. And Seymour already has a good start on the illustrations.

Perfect. Now, what about the other matter?

What other matter?

Our living arrangement. Don't you remember that I asked you to think of a way for Seymour, you, and me to live here together legally? Les and Diane Hope will arrive in Ghastly tomorrow to pick up Seymour. What can we do to stop them?

I have an idea. Please review the paperwork on the dining room table. I'll ask Seymour to do the same. If you both agree to the terms, we'll go to the courthouse tomorrow morning at 10 o'clock.

Petition to Adopt

Ghastly County Courthouse

I, Ignatius B. Grumply, a single person, and I, Olive C. Spence, a free spirit, request permission to adopt Seymour Hope.

We are submitting to the Court a letter from Les and Diane Hope dated October 14. This letter proves that their desire to reclaim Seymour is based not on their love for him but on his potential usefulness in marketing their new book.

We respectfully ask the Court to let Seymour decide with whom he wants to live, and advise the Court that if Seymour wishes to live with us, we would be honored to call him our son.

Ignatius B. Grumply

Ignatius B. Grumply

Olive C. Spence

Olive C. Spence

ADOPTION APPROVED

OCTOBER 31

Filed in the Circuit Court of Ghastly County

Judge Claire Voyant

Judge Claire Voyant
Ghastly Circuit Court

Saturday, November 1
Cliff Hanger, Editor

50 cents
Afternoon Edition

Seymour Hope Adopted by Grumply, Spence

Seymour Hope is now the legal son of Ignatius B. Grumply and Olive C. Spence.

So ruled Ghastly Circuit Court Judge Claire Voyant yesterday morning after reviewing the evidence. Judge Voyant said the testimonies by Grumply and Spence were especially convincing.

"Ms. Spence communicated with me by writing messages on my computer," said Voyant. "She testified that Seymour is a wonderful boy who deserves to be raised by parents who love him."

Grumply presented Judge Voyant with a letter written by Les and Diane Hope to Seymour Hope, who the couple thought was posing as Spence. After reviewing the letter, Judge Voyant terminated the parental rights of Les and Diane Hope and charged the couple with criminal child negligence.

"But we love our son," said Diane Hope.

"Even if we didn't, we have the right to use him to promote our new book," added Les Hope.

"Over my dead body!" said Judge Voyant, pounding her gavel. Voyant then asked Seymour Hope if he wished to be adopted by Spence and Grumply.

"Of course!" replied Hope. "They practically saved my life."

Grumply told Voyant that, in fact, Hope was largely responsible for rescuing him from the asylum.

"Seymour's plan saved my life and my sanity," explained Grumply.

Seymour Hope exits courthouse with his new parents.

"I couldn't have done it without Olive's help," Hope corrected.

"And Seymour and Iggy saved me from a deathly boring afterlife," Spence wrote on the judge's computer. "Isn't it crystal clear that we three belong together?"

Judge Voyant agreed. In her ruling she also approved Seymour Hope's home-schooling arrangement with Grumply and Spence.

Minutes later the happy trio emerged arm in arm in invisible arm from the courthouse.

"This is the coolest day of my life!" said Hope.

Ghastly Celebrates Halloween with Tricks, Treats and a Ghostlike Ghost Story

Forget burning books. Residents of Ghastly celebrated Halloween with a much hotter event: three new chapters from the serialized ghost story titled *43 Old Cemetery Road,* handed out by two of the creators at the Victorian mansion where they first met.

Coauthor Ignatius B. Grumply and his son, illustrator Seymour Hope, distributed copies of the new chapters from the front porch. Asked if Ms. Spence was available for comment, Grumply said: "Sorry, but it's been a long day for Olive. She wanted to enjoy watching the trick-or-treaters from her cupola, as she's done for decades."

The Halloween edition of *43 Old Cemetery Road* included both tricks and treats.

"We printed these new chapters in invisible ink," explained Grumply. "We also attached a small envelope containing itching powder to the page where Olive meets Dick Tater at her gravesite."

"Olive found a bunch of tricks in her coffin that we couldn't resist using," added a giggling Hope, who passed out invisible-ink decoder pens to readers, along with anti-itch cream to use as needed.

As for treats, last night's visitors to 43 Old Cemetery Rd. were invited inside the mansion, where the opulent dining room was outfitted with a Halloween buffet that

Trick-or-treaters pick up new chapters of a true ghost story.

included marshmallow soufflés, a chocolate fountain and a dip-your-own-caramel-apple station.

"I grew up trick-or-treating at Spence Mansion," said Fay Tality, president of the Bank of Ghastly. "But this is definitely the best Halloween ever!"

Like most guests Tality stayed at Spence Mansion until well after midnight. Before departing Tality yelled in the direction of the cupola: "Thank you, Olive! I can't wait to go home and read the new chapters! Oh, and I'm sorry I doubted you even for a moment!"

Kid Committee Convened to Abolish IMSPOOKY

A committee of middle grade students has convened to begin proceedings aimed at dismantling the International Movement for the Safety & Protection Of Our Kids & Youth (IMSPOOKY).

Called the Worldwide Committee of Kids Who Wish Their Parents Would Lighten Up a Bit & Quit Worrying So Much About Every Little Thing (WCK-WWTPWLUBQWSMAELT), the group urges children to help their parents relax by providing them with kind words, unasked-for favors and regular doses of chocolate.

A Message to Our Readers

Thank you for supporting our work at 43 Old Cemetery Road. We plan to keep writing, illustrating and publishing new chapters for as long as readers are interested, which we hope will be a very, very long time.

Olive C. Spence
Coauthor

Ignatius B. Grumply
Coauthor

Seymour Hope
Illustrator

Tater Confined Indefinitely

Tater is living at the Illinois Home for the Deranged.

Until further notice Dick Tater will remain at the Illinois Home for the Deranged.

If and when Tater is released from the facility, he won't return to Washington, D.C., as director of the International Movement for the Safety & Protection Of Our Kids & Youth. Tater was fired for using public funds to order five million copies of the now discredited book *Only Fools (and Children) Believe in Ghosts: The Authoritative Anti-Ghost Story* by Les and Diane Hope.

The professors are being held in the Ghastly County Jail, pending their trials on charges of criminal child negligence.

Les and Diane Hope are behind bars in the Ghastly County Jail.

And so, in a sense, we end where we began . . .
in a 32½-room house
built by a woman who,
in her lifetime, never married
or had children . . .
and rented by a man
who never married
and always thought he
disliked children . . .
and purchased by
a boy whose parents
abandoned him.

Except that now this house is the legal domicile of a new family, whose love for one another has been tested and proven . . .
Ghastly Courthouse
and whose legitimacy has been recognized by a court of law.
And so, even though one member of the family might still get grumpy now and then . . .

and another
might become
cranky when
she misplaces
her glasses . . .
neither would ever,
could ever,
abandon
Hope.

And that is why this 32½-room house at 43 Old Cemetery Road is now, once again . . .
43
a home.

The End

SEYMOUR HOPE

Illustrator in Residence

43 Old Cemetery Road
Third Floor
Ghastly, Illinois

November 1

Dear Olive,

I like the ending. But I think we forgot something.

Aren't readers going to wonder what happened to your old manuscripts?

Love,

—Seymour

Ghost Writer in Residence
43 Old Cemetery Road, The Cupola
Ghastly, Illinois

November 1

Dear Seymour,

You're absolutely right, dear. My mind is so full of cobwebs these days. I forgot something else, too.

I'll take care of both matters immediately.

Love,

Olive

Sunday, November 2
Cliff Hanger, Editor

$1.50
Morning Edition

Ghastly Public Library Receives Original Spence Manuscripts

The Ghastly Public Library received a unique donation yesterday: the unpublished manuscripts of Olive C. Spence.

The original manuscripts, which were delivered to the library in a coffin, were accompanied by a letter from Spence to chief librarian M. Balm.

"I never thanked you properly for the use of your bookmobile last week," wrote Spence. "I apologize for the inconvenience and my somewhat reckless driving. I hope you can understand why we were in such a hurry. I also want to thank you for refusing to burn books. You are a true friend to readers and writers everywhere."

According to Balm, the donation includes more than 200 unpublished mysteries.

"I'm dying to read them all," said Balm, "starting with *Mystery of the Missing Manuscripts*."

Balm sorts library's new collection.

Balm plans to display all of the manuscripts in the library, along with the letter from Spence.

"I wish I could thank Miss Spence for her generous donation," said Balm. "Olive, if you're reading this, please know how truly grateful I am. And don't worry about borrowing the bookmobile. I was happy to be of assistance!"

Anonymous Letter to be Investigated

Judge Voyant examines anonymous letter.

The anonymous letter that launched Dick Tater's investigation of 43 Old Cemetery Rd. is now in court custody.

"People have the right to send anonymous letters," said Ghastly Circuit Court Judge Claire Voyant. "But I want our prosecutor to investigate this letter to make sure no foul play was involved."

According to Voyant, the anonymous letter-writer used a rare font not found on modern computers.

IGNATIUS B. GRUMPLY

A WRITER IN RESIDENCE

43 OLD CEMETERY ROAD　　2ND FLOOR　　GHASTLY, ILLINOIS

November 2

Olive C. Spence
The Cupola
43 Old Cemetery Road
Ghastly, Illinois

Dear Olive,

You wrote that anonymous letter to Dick Tater, didn't you? I know because only you use a font that

Of course I wrote the letter.

Why?

I wanted to show the world what a relentless busybody Mr. Tater is.

Some people might call *you* a busybody.

How can I be a busybody when I no longer have a body?

I believe I've noted this fact in a previous conversation.

Maybe you have, dear. I'm sorry. I've been terribly distracted by all this Tater turmoil. I never intended for things to get so out of hand. I only wanted to put Tater in his place and bring Les and Diane Hope to justice. Please believe me when I tell you that I had *no* idea you and Seymour would be taken away in the process.

I do believe you, Olive.

Thank goodness. Now, Iggy, dare I mention there's another reason I wrote that letter to Tater?

I think I know, but tell me anyway.

I wanted Seymour to live with parents who love him.

And you thought it wouldn't occur to me to try to adopt him?

Well, Iggy, you *can* be a little slow some-times.

Would it surprise you to know that I was working on the adoption papers the day Dick Tater's first letter arrived?

Oh, Iggy! You are a treasure. You'll make a wonderful father to Seymour.

Thank you. But sometimes I fear I really am deranged. Falling in love with a ghost? Adopting a child—at my age? The whole thing feels a bit crazy.

The best things in life usually do, dear. Now go to bed. It's late.

I know. See you tomorrow. (I wish.)

You really *do* wish you could see me, don't you?

Yes, Olive, I *do*. I've seen you only once in my life, and it was just a glance.

All right, all right. But make it quick. I'm in my robe and slippers, and my hair is in rollers. This is *not* my best look. But here you go. What? What?! Iggy, say something. *Write* something. You're making me nervous with that silly look on your face. Are you just going to sit there with your mouth hanging open and *stare* at me? Very well, then. The show's over. Are you happy now?

Olive . . . you're beautiful.

Yes I am, darling. I'm also dead tired. Good night, Iggy.

Good night, Olive.

Good night, reader.

The *Real* End

(for now, anyway)

Other books written by Kate Klise and illustrated by M. Sarah Klise:

Dying to Meet You: 43 Old Cemetery Road

Regarding the Fountain
Regarding the Sink
Regarding the Trees
Regarding the Bathrooms
Regarding the Bees

Letters from Camp
Trial by Journal

Shall I Knit You a Hat?
Why Do You Cry?
Imagine Harry
Little Rabbit and the Night Mare

Also written by Kate Klise:

Deliver Us from Normal
Far from Normal

A Very Ghastly Halloween
Ignatius B. Grumply
as a
Work in Progress
Seymour Hope
as a
Famous Artist
Shadow
as
Puss 'n Boots
Judge Clai
as the
Statue of Liberty
Tality
as a
Grown-up Pirate